Leave me alone!

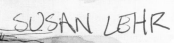

SUSAN LEHR

THE Moon Clock

WRITTEN AND ILLUSTRATED BY

MATT FAULKNER

SCHOLASTIC INC.

NEW YORK

Dedicated to all my friends
who helped in making
The Moon Clock what it is.

—MF

"Wherever you go,
there you are."

—BUCKAROO BANZAI

Library of Congress Cataloging-in-Publication Data

Faulkner, Matt.
The moonclock/by Matt Faulkner.
p.   cm.
Summary: A young girl journeys to a faraway place and finds the
inner strength to confront the bullies of other worlds and her own.
ISBN 0–590–41593–X:
[1. Fantasy   2. Bullies—Fiction.]   I. Title.
PZ7.F2765Mo   1991
[E]—dc20   91-99
                                    CIP
                                    AC

12 11 10 9 8 7 6 5 4 3 2 1   1 2 3 4 5 6/9

Printed in the U.S.A.

First Scholastic printing, October 1991   36

Design by Claire Counihan

Tricky typesetting by the Sarabande Press

The illustrations were done with ink drawings over watercolor washes.

As the morning sun rose, slender shafts of sunshine crawled across Robin's bedroom floor and came to rest upon a small trunk, a present from her dad, who was far away on a business trip.

Wake up!

Robin pretended to be sick so she could stay home from school. Feeling sorry for herself, she turned to her dolls, hoping to find a friendly pair of eyes smiling back at her. But she was out of luck. They all happened to be sick that day, too.

Perched on top of the tiny trunk, Rotunda tried to get Robin's attention.

What's up, Rotunda?

Let's have a look inside the trunk.

Robin knelt down and gave the key a twist.

Terribly sorry if I frightened you, but I'm in a dreadful hurry. My name's Kolshinsky, and I've been sent to find a hero. I'm looking for someone brave, someone fearless.

Once
inside
the trunk,
they
found a
DOOR.

Where are we? What's happening? How do we get down?

No time for questions. **The enemy is at our gate.**

They raced through the city.

I can't wake them up.

Zzz

I have an **idea.**

I'll sing to them.

How will that help?

This ought to be good for a few laughs.

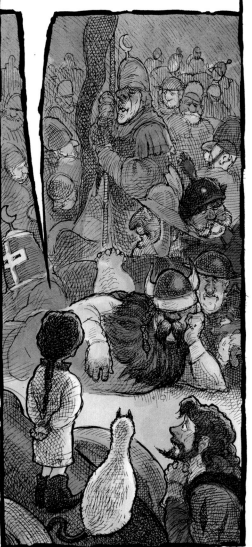

I learned this song in school. I hope you like it.

Suddenly, the soldiers were awake.

The armies clashed!

Pillows?

Robin

handled her weapon with great skill.

And the celebration began . . .

Hurry! Your mother's **coming.** Let's get out of here.

Open up, Robin. I've got lunch.

Okay, Mom.

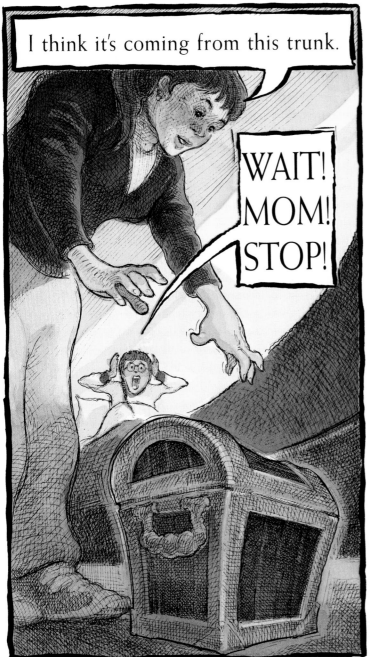

I think it's coming from this trunk.

WAIT! MOM! STOP!

I can't watch.

Oh my, Rotunda.

Reooow.

Umph.

SPROING

Oh, it's only you.

Hmmph.